Those
DARN
Squirrels
and the
CAT NEXT DOOR

by
Adam Rubin
Illustrated by
Daniel Salmieri

Houghton Mifflin Harcourt
Boston New York

For the cats: the one who chirped, the one
who squawked, and the one who said
my name—generous gift givers all.
—A.R.

For Grandma — I love you.
—D.S.

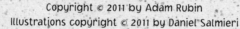

www.hmhco.com

The text was set in 16-point Jacoby ICG Light.
The illustrations were executed in watercolor, gouache, and colored pencil.

The Library of Congress has cataloged the hardcover as follows:
Rubin, Adam, 1983–
Those darn squirrels and the cat next door/by Adam Rubin; illustrated by Daniel Salmieri.
p. cm.
Summary: Grumpy Old Man Fookwire's new neighbor has a cat that threatens his beloved birds,
but the pesky squirrels figure out a way to solve the problem.
[1. Squirrels—Fiction. 2. Birds—Fiction. 3. Cats—Fiction. 4. Neighbors—Fiction. 5. Humorous Stories.]
I. Salmieri, Daniel, 1983– ill. II.Title.
PZ7.R83116Ti 2011
[E]—dc22

ISBN: 978-0-547-42922-9 hardcover
ISBN: 978-0-544-80402-4 paperback

Manufactured in China
SCP 10 9 8 7 6 5 4 3 2 1
4500599999

Old Man Fookwire lived on the edge of the forest just outside town. He was a terrible grump, and in the wintertime, he was even grumpier than usual. Whenever it snowed, he would shut his eyes tight and think of summer. He missed sunshine, suntan lotion, and weenie roasts. But most of all he missed the birds who flew south when it got cold.

During the long, lonely winter months, the only critters left in Fookwire's backyard were squirrels.

Now, not many people know this, but squirrels are the champions of the forest.

They are craftier than beavers, smarter than foxes, and swifter than rabbits. They are also full of mischief.

When it got too cold outside, the squirrels would drop in through Fookwire's mail slot and visit him at home. They'd warm themselves by the fire and finish the old man's crossword puzzles.

When Fookwire woke up, he'd chase them out with a broom. Then he'd shake his old-man fist and yell, "Those darn squirrels!"

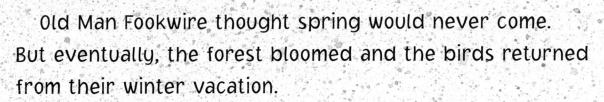

Old Man Fookwire thought spring would never come. But eventually, the forest bloomed and the birds returned from their winter vacation.

Whirley birds chomped on tumbleberries. Bonga birds snacked on honey snaps. And the floogle bird ate farfle seeds until he got so full, he had to lie down.

Fookwire danced through the yard with delight. He set up his easel and brushes. Then he painted the birds till he got blisters on his fingers.

Tired and happy, the old man went inside for a quiet afternoon snack.

Suddenly . . .

KABOOM!

Old Man Fookwire spilled cottage cheese all over his suspenders.

KABLAM!

The floogle bird fell out of his nest.

KABLOOEY!

The squirrels had to restart their annual chess tournament.

The noise was coming from the house across the stream. It was the sound of a small woman unloading enormous crates and moving in.

Fookwire's new neighbor was Little Old Lady Hu, the town baker. The only thing sweeter than the pies Hu baked was the little old lady herself. Everyone in town loved her. But no one could stand her cat, Muffins. He was a real jerk.

Hu didn't see things that way. She thought Muffins was a cuddly honey bunny. But after the infamous poodle incident, she'd decided to move to the forest so that her cat could make some new friends.

After unpacking her crates, Little Old Lady Hu baked a
tumbleberry pie. Then she and Muffins went to say hello
to their new neighbor.

Fookwire despised conversation, so he hid behind the drapes.
The squirrels were scared of the cat, so they hid inside the
drainpipes. The birds weren't sure why everyone was hiding,
but they stuffed themselves down the chimney just to be safe.

Eventually, Hu got tired of waiting for Fookwire to answer the door.
She walked around front, pushed the pie through the mail slot, and
went home.

Normally, Old Man Fookwire hated pie, but this one smelled delicious. He took a deep whiff and closed his eyes. When he opened them, the squirrels were licking the plate clean.

"Those darn squirrels!" shouted Fookwire.

Full and happy, the squirrels stumbled from
the house—where Muffins ambushed them.

The dastardly cat grabbed one
squirrel and gave him a wet willy.

He snatched another and
gave her a noogie.

Then he tied two squirrels'
tails together.

Luckily, Little Old Lady Hu returned before Muffins could do more. She scooped him up and scratched him under the chin. "Come now, shnookums," she cooed. "It's time for dinner. You can play with your new friends another day."

The next morning, Muffins burst into the yard, terrifying the birds and interrupting Old Man Fookwire's painting. Then the sneaky cat pounced on an unsuspecting group of squirrels and gave them all wedgies—not an easy thing to do, because generally squirrels do not wear underpants.

The squirrels were furious. The birds flew up to the treetops and refused to come down. And Old Man Fookwire was so upset, he wrote a letter to the mayor to complain about his new neighbors.

FOOKWIRE
A MEMOIR

That night the squirrels held a meeting to figure out what to do about the cat next door. They ate cheese puffs and drank ginger ale to help them think. Finally they had it: the perfect plan.

When Muffins came over the next day, the birds were feeding peacefully beneath a tree. A wicked smile came over the cat's fluffy face. He wriggled his haunches and launched himself through the air.

The frightened birds swooped into the sky, yanking the strings the squirrels had tied to their tail feathers. The strings sprang the trap, and the cat was doused with a gallon of freezing cold water.

Muffins let out a furious yowl.

Old Man Fookwire ran outside when he heard the terrible noise. "Great googley-moogley!" he exclaimed. "That pathetic wretch is no bigger than a squirrel!"

It was true! Underneath all his fluff and fuzz, Muffins was nothing but a skinnymalink. He lowered his head in embarrassment and sloshed his way home as fast as he could.

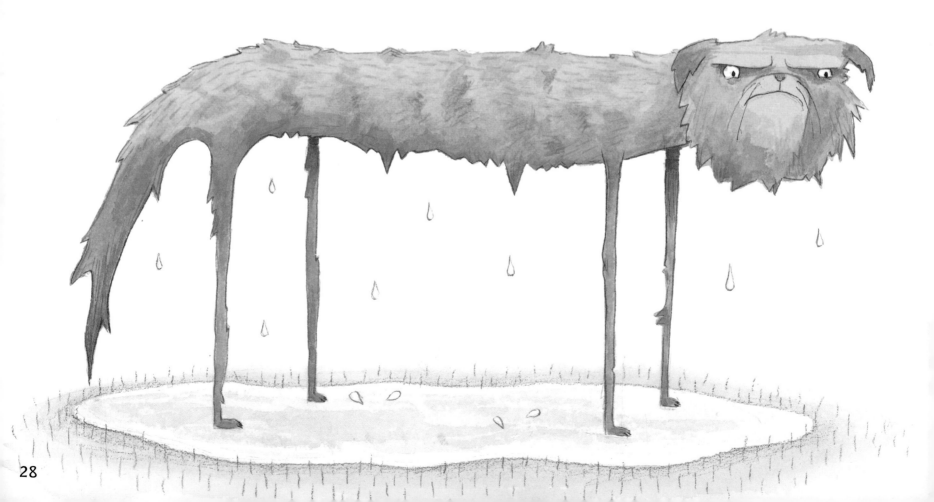

The squirrels' plan had worked perfectly.
They gave each other high-fives. The baba
birds snickered, the yaba birds chuckled,
and the floogle bird enjoyed a hearty guffaw.
Fookwire snapped his suspenders with delight.
"Those darn squirrels," he said fondly.

Old Man Fookwire never warmed up to his new neighbors. He was a grump, after all. But Little Old Lady Hu became quite good chums with the birds and squirrels. Each Saturday when the bakery closed, she brought all the unsold cakes and pies and cookies home. She set them out on her picnic table, and everyone gathered for a delicious, fun-filled feast.

Everyone except the cat next door, who refused
to leave the house ever again.